LULU
and the
WITCH BABY

An I Can Read Book®

LULU
and the
WITCH BABY

Jane O'Connor

Pictures by
Emily Arnold McCully

A Harper Trophy Book
Harper & Row, Publishers

Lulu and the Witch Baby
Text copyright © 1986 by Jane O'Connor
Illustrations copyright © 1986 by Emily Arnold McCully
All rights reserved. No part of this book may be
used or reproduced in any manner whatsoever without
written permission except in the case of brief quotations
embodied in critical articles and reviews. Printed in
the United States of America. For information address
Harper & Row Junior Books, 10 East 53rd Street,
New York, N.Y. 10022.

Library of Congress Cataloging-in-Publication Data
O'Connor, Jane.
Lulu and the witch baby.

(An I can read book)
Summary: Lulu Witch begins to change her mind about
her pesky baby sister when she thinks that one of her
magic spells has made the baby disappear.
[1. Witches—Fiction.   2. Sisters—Fiction]
I. McCully, Emily Arnold, ill.   II. Title.   III. Series.
PZ7.0222Lu 1986   [E]   85-45832
ISBN 0-06-024626-X
ISBN 0-06-024627-8 (lib. bdg.)
ISBN 0-06-444130-X (pbk.)

First Harper Trophy edition, 1989.

For Robby and Teddy

Everybody loved Witch Baby.

Everybody but Lulu Witch.

She did not love Witch Baby at all.

It was not fair.

Witch Baby got all the presents—

a cuddly dragon from Granny,

a bat rattle from Aunt Boo Boo,

8

a witch doll with a broomstick
from Cousin Hazel,
and a Dracula-in-the-box
from Uncle Fuzzy.

It was not fair.

Nobody ever had time

for Lulu Witch anymore.

"Mama! Mama!" cried Lulu Witch.

"Watch me fly on my broom."

"Not now, dear," said Mama Witch.

"I am busy."

"Papa! Papa!

Please fix my dollhouse,"

said Lulu Witch.

"Not now, dear," said Papa Witch.

"I am busy."

It was not fair.

Nobody ever got mad

at Witch Baby.

Not even when she was bad.

And she was bad a lot.

Witch Baby was always

pulling Spot's tail.

Witch Baby was always

messing up Lulu's things.

And one time Witch Baby

even spit food at Lulu Witch.

"Witch Baby is just a baby,"

said Mama Witch.

"She thinks it is funny."

"Some joke," said Lulu Witch.

She wished Witch Baby would go away.

She wished Witch Baby would go away

forever.

Then one day Lulu got her wish.

It was a rainy day.

Lulu was drawing with her crayons.

Mama Witch said,

"I must go to market.

Will you watch Witch Baby?"

"Yes, Mama," said Lulu Witch.

"And do not go to the magic room,"

said Mama Witch.

"Yes, Mama," said Lulu Witch.

"I will be back soon,"

said Mama Witch.

And away she flew.

Lulu went back to her drawing.

It was a drawing

of a mother witch

and a little girl witch.

They were holding hands.

Lulu drew stars on their dresses,

and pointy hats on their heads,

and little warts on their noses.

It was the best drawing

Lulu Witch had ever done.

She could not wait

to show it to Mama Witch.

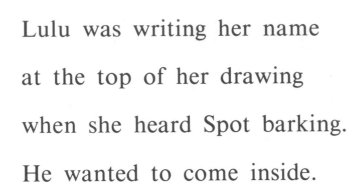

Lulu was writing her name
at the top of her drawing
when she heard Spot barking.
He wanted to come inside.

"I hear you, boy,"

Lulu called to Spot.

"I will let you in."

Lulu Witch went to the front door

and opened it.

21

Spot jumped up on Lulu.

He licked her face.

"Good boy! Good boy!"

said Lulu.

Spot looked hungry.

So Lulu gave him

a bowl of Monster Yummies.

Then Lulu Witch

went back to her room.

Oh no!

There was Witch Baby.

And there was the drawing.

In lots of little pieces!

Witch Baby smiled at Lulu,

and said, "Goo goo!"

She was not even sorry.

25

"I hate you, Witch Baby!"

shouted Lulu Witch.

"I hate you more

than eating lizard liver.

I hate you more

than having a bad dream.

I hate you more

than getting a shot.

I wish you would go away forever!"

All at once

Lulu thought of the magic room

and the magic book of spells.

Maybe a spell

would make Witch Baby go away.

Mama Witch had told Lulu

not to go to the magic room.

But Lulu Witch went anyway.

Lulu Witch found the magic book.

It was very big and very heavy.

Lulu put the book in her lap

and turned the pages.

"Here is what I need," she said.

"This will make

Witch Baby go away."

Slowly, Lulu read

the disappearing spell.

Mix together

5 drops of bat blood

8 fly legs

1 cup of snake guts

2 cups of swamp water

17 hairs from a black cat.

Lulu worked fast.

She got a big bowl

and a spoon.

She got a bottle of bat blood,

a bottle of fly legs,

a bottle of snake guts,

a bottle of swamp water,

and a bottle of hairs

from a black cat.

Lulu put everything in the big bowl.

"Drat!" she said.

"I need seventeen cat hairs.

There are only sixteen cat hairs

in the bottle."

Lulu hoped the spell

would work anyway.

Lulu stirred the magic stuff

with the spoon.

It turned brown and smelled funny.

"It looks ready to me,"

said Lulu Witch,

and she ran back to her room.

Witch Baby was busy

breaking all Lulu's crayons.

Lulu Witch did not care.

She sprinkled the magic stuff

on Witch Baby's head.

"Good-bye, Witch Baby!" she shouted.

Lulu Witch closed her eyes
and counted to ten.
Then she opened her eyes.
Witch Baby was still there.
"Maybe I have to say
some magic words,"
thought Lulu Witch.

She sprinkled more magic stuff

on Witch Baby's head.

Then she said,

"Hocus pocus!

Hip hip hooray!

Witch Baby! Witch Baby!

Go away!"

40

But Witch Baby was still there.

"Drat!" said Lulu Witch.

"The spell is not working,

because there were

only sixteen cat hairs."

Lulu Witch ran back

to the magic room.

She washed the bowl and the spoon.

She put away the magic book.

She put away all the bottles.

She had to clean up fast,

before Mama Witch got home.

42

Then Lulu Witch

hurried back to her room.

Great goblins!

Witch Baby was gone!

The spell had worked!

"Hooray!" shouted Lulu Witch.

"No more Witch Baby!"

Lulu Witch danced around the room.

She gave Spot a hug.

Then Lulu Witch

thought about Mama Witch.

Mama Witch was *not* going to be happy

that Witch Baby was gone.

Mama Witch was going to be mad.

Very, very mad!

Lulu Witch stopped dancing.

"Maybe I better

bring back Witch Baby,"

Lulu Witch said.

She ran down

to the magic room again.

Lulu Witch

got out the magic book.

She found a spell

to stop a cold,

and a spell

to turn a frog into a prince,

and even a spell

to make gold out of straw.

But no spell

to bring back Witch Baby.

Lulu Witch got scared.

Where *was* Witch Baby?

Was Witch Baby all alone?

Was Witch Baby scared?

Lulu Witch started to cry.

"I am a very wicked witch,"
she said.

"I wish I had never made that spell.
I wish Witch Baby was back."

Lulu Witch wished

as hard as she could.

She crossed all her fingers

and all her toes.

Then she made up

some more magic words.

"Hocus pocus,

flipper flapperjack,

Witch Baby, Witch Baby,

please come back!"

Lulu Witch hoped

her magic words would work.

She ran back to see.

There was Witch Baby!

"I did it!" cried Lulu Witch.

"I am a big girl witch.

I can make spells.

I can say magic words."

Witch Baby smiled at Lulu Witch

and said, "Goo goo."

Lulu Witch gave

Witch Baby a kiss.

"You are just a baby," she said.

"What a nice big sister!"

said Mama Witch.

"You are back!"

cried Lulu Witch.

"Yes," said Mama Witch.

"When I came home,

Witch Baby was a mess.

There was sticky brown stuff

all over her.

I took her into the bathroom

to wash her off."

"OH!" cried Lulu Witch.

The magic spell

had not worked after all.

Deep down Lulu was glad.

"I was looking for you,"

Mama Witch told Lulu.

"Where were you?"

Lulu Witch looked down

at her shoes.

"I was looking

for Witch Baby," she said.

That was not really the truth.

But it was not really a lie.

"Look what I bought,"

said Mama Witch.

"A toadstool pie, your favorite."

Mama Witch and Lulu Witch

ate the toadstool pie.

They left a piece for Papa Witch.

Witch Baby

had a bottle of baby brew.

She was too little to eat pie.

She was just a baby!